Victor R

A Masonic Poem

Harriet Annie Wilkins

Alpha Editions

This edition published in 2024

ISBN : 9789362926500

Design and Setting By
Alpha Editions
www.alphaedis.com
Email - info@alphaedis.com

As per information held with us this book is in Public Domain.
This book is a reproduction of an important historical work. Alpha Editions uses the best technology to reproduce historical work in the same manner it was first published to preserve its original nature. Any marks or number seen are left intentionally to preserve its true form.

Contents

Preface..- 1 -
Victor's Soliloquy. ....- 2 -
Robert's Death. ....- 8 -
Ethel's Mission. ....- 14 -
Aimee's Soliloquy. ....- 17 -
Twelve Month's After. ....- 23 -
Miscellaneous Pieces Mist and Sunshine. ....- 29 -
Charge to the Knight of Malta ....- 31 -
The Curl of Gold. ....- 33 -
Holy Communion. ....- 35 -
Song of Azael. ....- 37 -
Only a Story ....- 40 -
Daybreak. ....- 42 -
The Wife's Watch. ....- 43 -
Adoniram. ....- 45 -
Songs in the Night. ....- 47 -
In Memoriam. ....- 49 -
A Song of the Flowers. ....- 51 -
The Cities of Old. ....- 53 -
Out of His Time. ....- 55 -
Two Altars. ....- 57 -
The Doom of Cain. ....- 59 -
Our Poor Brethren. ....- 61 -
Vain Dreams. ....- 63 -
The Forest River. ....- 65 -
Last Words of Sir Henry Lawrence. ....- 67 -

To the Birds..- 69 -
Initiation Ode. ....- 70 -
Installation Ode. ....- 71 -

Preface

An anecdote appeared some time ago in the pages of "The Craftsman" which gave rise to the ideas embodied in "Victor Roy." It is not a story of profound depth. Its aim is not to soar to Alpine heights of imagination, or to excavate undiscovered treasures from the mines of thought. It is a very simple story, told in very simple words, of such lives as are around us in our midst. It tells of sorrows that are daily being borne by suffering humanity, and of the faith that gives strength to that suffering humanity to endure "seeing Him, who is invisible." All lives may not see their earth day close in sunshine, but somewhere the sun is shining, and all true cross-bearers shall some day become true crown-wearers. The following pages have some references to that Ancient Order which comes down the centuries, bearing upon its structure the marks of that Grand Master Builder, who gave to the visible universe "the sun to rule the day, the moon and stars to govern the night;" an Order which, like these wondrous orbs, is grand in its mysterious symbolism, calm in its unvarying circles, universal in its beneficence.

We are told of a poor weary traveller who had plucked a flower. The shadows of a grand cathedral lay before him. He entered; its architecture charmed him, its calmness refreshed him. Approaching a shrine he laid his flower upon it, saying: "It is all I can give; it, too, is God's work, although gathered by a feeble, dying hand." A priest standing near looked upon the flower and said: "God bless you, my brother, heaven is nearer to me." So, if by the perusal of "Victor Roy" one ear hears more distinctly the Apostolic declaration, "Pure religion is to visit the fatherless and widows in their affliction," or if one poor sinking spirit is strengthened, as Longfellow says, to "touch God's right hand in the darkness," the wishes of the Authoress will be fully accomplished.

Harriett Annie

Hamilton, August, 1882.

Victor's Soliloquy.

Heavily rolleth the wintry clouds,
   And the ceaseless snow is falling, falling,
As the frost king's troops in their icy shrouds,
   Whistle and howl, like lost spirits calling.

But a warm luxuriantly furnished room,
   Is an antidote to the wild night storm,
Lamplight and firelight banish the gloom,
   No poverty stalks there with cold gaunt form.

Yet there seems a shadow, yes even there,
   Where all is so peacefully grand and still,
No fair young face with its shining hair,
   No voice of love with its musical thrill.

One reigneth alone in that mansion grand,
   And his day of life has long past its noon,
The wanderer of many a foreign land,
   Rests, calmly waiting Heaven's final boon.

There are lines on his brow of grief and care,
   Writ with a quill from Time's feathered wing.
There are silver threads in the chesnut hair,
   The blossoms white of a fair dawning spring.

Yet Victor Roy has a kindly word,
   And a kindly smile for all he meets;
No cry of distress is by him unheard,
   While many a blessing his pathway greets.

"Yes, that's right Jasper, draw the curtains close,
And make the fire burn bright;
God help the poor and suffering ones
Within this city to-night.
Did your wife send food to that sick girl in the market lane to-day?
Did you carry coals to the man whose limbs were crushed by the loaded dray?
Well, that's all right, what is it you say? you wish that I did but know
The comfort I give to hearts that are weak, or erring or low.
Have you turned lecturer, Jasper? no; but it makes you sad,
To see me lonely and quiet when I'm making others glad.
But Jasper, remember that you and I, hold certain things in trust,
We must gain some interest on our gold, not let it lie and rust.
I am but a steward for the King, till the time of his return,

There, that will do, supper at ten; how bright those fresh coals burn."
Poor Jasper, he thinks me moping and sad; well, well, I only know
I do not wish that he or aught should ever consider me so,
It would seem like base ingratitude to the Ruler of my way,
Who showers His blessings about and around me every day.
But oh, Great Architect, whose hand has carved my destiny,
There was a time when in my pride, I owned not Thine nor Thee,
Unheeding the Holy Light Divine to man's dark pathway sent,
Unheeding the Bible, blessed chart, to storm tossed sailors sent;
With a film in my eyes, I would not see the ladder based on earth,
Yet reaching to the cloud-crowned height, where the true Light has birth.
The beautiful angels passing up, with all our prayers to God,
Our tears and moans, our fading flowers, all stained with mire and sod--
And coming down; ah, many a time I have blessed the Lord above,
For His pure descending angels, bringing Faith, and Hope, and Love.
There was a time when all this wealth of glory was lost on me,
And I was like a rudderless ship, far out on the rocking sea,
I had a friend, oh that blessed word, we had been parted for years,
And I wandered one day to find him, my heart had no cloudy fears.
That day stands out in bold relief upon Memory's wreck-strewn shore,
Like a beacon light in the lighthouse, undimned by the rush and roar.
'Twas a day in the early June, the clover was red in the field,
And the zephyrs garnered the kisses, the gentle violets yield.
Birds sang, and the sunshine flickered out and about through the cloud,
What had a day like that to do with a pall, a coffin, a shroud?
I stood in a flower-decked churchyard, and on the procession came,
Why did I ask to be answered back, that his was the sleeper's name,
Nearer now to the dark brown earth the band of his brothers turned,
And on snowy aprons and collars of blue the merry sunbeams burned,
I, like a suddenly petrified stone, stood mid the crowd that day,
And with ears which seemed to be leaden, I listened and heard one say:

> "Brother, we have met before,
> Where the Tyler guards the door,
> We have given the well-known sign,
> That has blent our souls with thine,
> Now this eve, thou giv'st no word,
> Back to our souls deep stired,
> For the Angel Tylers wait,
> At thy Lodge Room's mystic gate.
>
> "Brother, thou art taking rest,
> We must still the wild storm breast,
> We must build through mist and night,

Thou hast seen the quenchless Light,
While we hew the shapeless stone,
Thou hast bowed before the Throne,
While we tread the chequered floor,
Thou hast pass'd the golden door.

"Oh Companion, were we there,
Ended every pleading prayer,
Ended all the work and toil,
Gathered all the fruit and spoil,
Finished all the war of sin,
By the Warden's hand shut in,
Brother; once again with thee,
What would our first greeting be?

"Loved Companions, we have given,
To the guardianship of Heaven,
Our Brother's precious dust,
And in memory of the just,
Be it ours still to guard,
All he loved, with watch and ward,
Till like him we reach a shore,
Where these sorrows come no more."

"All he loved," I knew as I stood there, he loved not one of that band
As we had loved in our boyhood days, heart to heart and hand to hand,
They called us David and Jonathan, for our hearts were knit as one,
And now I saw him left alone, in the shades of of the dying sun;
Was it his spirit beside me stood; for do not their spirits come,
Relieved from all burden of earthly dross, and win us up to their home?
Was it his spirit urged me on, to seek for the Orient Light?
It seemed that I should be nearer him if one in that mystic rite,
Never a Syrian ready to perish, needed more timely aid,
Never a pilgrim knocked at the door and found more restful shade,
Aye, time has carried me on some way, since the hour I saw the light,
And morning has gone, noontide has gone, now soon must draw on the night.
I heard the young lads in the office talking about me to-day,
I did not mean to play the part of eaves-dropper in their way,
They were wondering who in the name of fate, I would find for my heir,
Wondering why I never was married, there are some so proud and fair,
They knew I could have for the asking, and so they went on with their fun,
Till the "Senior Partner" gave a cough, and then all their mirth was done.
But I asked from Heaven though I know the way is mingled flower and thorn,

That not one from partner to porter may bear all I have borne.
So Jasper thinks I am sad; how the wintry winds whistle to-night!
Heaven grant no poor woman or children are out in this sleety blight.
I cannot read this eve; what ails me? "Chronicle," "Tribune" and "Times,"
Lie looking coaxingly at me, I heed not their prose or rhymes,
Is it thinking so much of Arthur, brings Aimee before me here,
Aimee, my idol, my darling, my pet, who always spoke words of cheer,
Did I say what brings her near me to-night, she is with me every day.
God help me, for Aimee's another man's wife three thousand miles away,
Oh how we loved! there's no use in talking, all do not love the same,
To some 'tis the bread and breath of life, to some it is only a name.
We were going to be married the coming spring, we had planned our nest,
Down in the fairest of fairy dells, in sight of the blue sea's breast,
When Uncle Roy who had sailed to India, many long years before,
Gone from the towers of Edinburgh, and made piles of golden store,
Sent for me all in a hurry and ere long he died on my breast,
And far from the land of the heather we laid him gently to rest.
And then came the fever to me, sick and weak at the point of death,
Raving for Aimee--they told me 'twas Aimee at every breath.
Weeks passed and I woke again one day to breath as it were new air.
The crisis over; now health, life, love and myself a millionaire.
But Victor Ellis came back no more, I was changed into Victor Roy.
Yes, a king with a crown of gold, but the gold was a broken toy,
For a letter lay by me from England, a strange hand-writing to me,
Telling me Aimee, my star of hope, was lost in the treacherous sea.
A party went boating one eve, and the pleasure boat struck the bar,
And before any help could be given, Aimee had floated out far.
Every available thing was done, that landsman or sailor could try,
So fell the burning shower of words that met my bewildered eye.
Oh the night at noon, I have wondered oft how much the heart will bear,
As strand after strand of the toughened cord, strains with the weight and wear.
I felt I must fly, weak as I was, to where she was lying; perhaps
'Twas a merciful Providence after all, that I took a relapse.
Oh the weary months that crawled slowly by at a tortoise creeping pace,
I seeming to hear the dash of the waves, that hid a beloved face.
Time passed, and I learnt that the roaring sea was not the treacherous thing.
'Twas not the dumb wave, but a living man that turned to Winter my Spring,
And Aimee had married another and sought the Australian shore.
She must have thought I was dead, Heaven help me, betwixt us ocean's roar.
I have sometimes wondered if gold is ever aught but a curse,

No, that's wrong--if honestly gained, no harm in a well filled purse,
But I often think of the little home standing there by the sea,
For far off merry England, the home planned for Aimee and me.
Oh to have toiled for her from dawn till the dews of restful night,
Her smile my guerdon, her love my prize, her heart so happy and bright.
Often I wonder if peace and love have sheltered her with their wings;
Of wealth I suppose they have plenty, and the comforts money brings,
For Montrose was the heir to a large amount of money I know,
And he certainly was not the kind of man to let his money go.
But there must be something warmer than gold to brighten Aimee's sky,
And I hav'nt much faith in a man who could win such a prize by a lie.
But Heaven is good that I found him not when my soul was passion rife,
'Twould only have brought her grief, for my aim was a life for a life,
Well-a-day! come here "Chronicle," let us see if you have a word
To calm the current of burning thoughts that down to their depths are stirred,
I'll read the first thing I meet with, murders, fires, or kingdoms riven;
Oh you are the first on the page, "Vera, to her lover in Heaven."

"My lover why is it this night of storms,
  My thoughts are ever turning to thee?
You who are sheltered from all the blast,
  Hear the murmuring sounds of the crystal sea.

"My lover; do you remember the day,
  When last my hands were in yours entwined,
And the air was faint with the summer flowers,
  While a roll of thunder came on the wind.

"My lover; who always spoke words of love,
  The tone of thy voice is so clear but far,
A bridge is between us I cannot cross,
  But God's will stands at each end of the bar.

"My lover; did you with your mist-cleared eyes,
  See me when I thought you were far away,
Did you bring down Hope from your new-found skies,
  While my heart was breaking over your clay?

"My lover; how long have the seasons been,
  Since I tried to spell out the small word 'wait,'
And learnt to know that your love and life,
  Grow ever more strong as the years grow late.

"My lover; in dreams of the night you come,
  Out of God's goodness sent from afar,

He arches the barriers for the best,
  And Christ's love stands at each end of the bar.

"Some day that arch will widen its breadth,
  There'll be room for two, you'll not come in vain,
And over the darkness of weeping and death,
  We'll be always together, and happy again."

Why did I read these lines, was it only to mock my woe?
For less would the burden be and the sin would be less I know,
If I knew that my darling was safe and blest where the angels are.
Why do I murmur? for God's will stands at each end of the mystic bar.
Well, why do I stay here gazing hopelessly into the fire?
Watching the coals that glow and burn, then fall away and expire,
It seems that out of their flashing light my lost love appears to rise,
And another face that has haunted me all day with its wistful eyes
As we halted at church to-day; a face, a young girl's face, so sad,
Looked out among the crowd that gazed, and her dark eyes made me glad.
What strange, queer beings we are, a look, or a song, or a flower,
A scent on the air, a sound of the sea, they come with such power,
That the long years vanish away, and over death's murky tide
Spiritual bodies fearlessly walk, and stand with us side by side.
Gone is all distance and time, vanished far is the grave's eclipse.
Again sweet voices are in our ears, their breath upon our lips,
So, with that poor, strange child to-day, who has never heard Aimee's name,
Little she thought that her earnest eyes rekindled a smouldering flame.
There was an old familiar look of the happy days once fled,
An old familiar look of one that I love as we love the dead.
Love her? love Aimee? do I love her less, because since I kissed her last
Over my desolate heart the tides of twenty-five years have passed?
I am longing to-night to hear her hymn, her sweet "Abide with me,"
As she sang it, leaning upon my breast the night I put out to sea.
I know it was only she I loved, and thought of that eventide;
But now I can fully endorse the draft, "O Lord with me abide,"
And spite of the heavy clouds that hang o'er my life path near and far,
I own with Vera that "Christ's love stands at each end of the mystic bar,"
And so much of the desert life has been travelled by night and day,
That the shores of the summer land are not so very far away.
And although I know there is one dark sea where black waves heave and toss,
I know the Pilot who waits for me will carry me safely across.
My path down to that water's edge is one avenue of pines;
But though I walk amid shadows dim, o'erhead the bright sun shines.

Robert's Death

Heavily rolleth the wintry clouds,
And the ceaseless snow is falling, falling,
While the frost king's troops in their icy shrouds
Whistle and howl like lost spirits calling.

In a scantily furnished tenement room.
Through which the same frost troops are sighing,
Churlishly gloweth the charcoal flame,
While a man lies there in penury dying.

Nothing new on this beautiful earth,
Are hunger and nakedness, cold and pain,
Over God's sinless creation of love
The serpent glides with his poisonous train.

"Where is Aimee?" here I lie all alone in this wretched hole,
I who was reared as a gentleman's son, an aristocrat to the soul,
Could drink more wine at my father's board than the best man out of a score;
Rode with the hounds at ten years old, and played high in a few years more.
A man can live without love, but he can't get along without gold,
And a woman and child sadly hamper a fellow that's poor or old.
How can a gentleman work and toil year after year like a slave?
For when you've worked your life away you're asked, "Why did not you save?"
Not that I would reproach my wife, I daresay she has done her best;
But women can earn such a trifle, and grow weak if they lose their rest.
Not that Aimee has ever grumbled, and I am not to be blamed,
If she choose to work and stitch away from morn till the sunset flamed;
And just the course of my crooked luck, that if but one child we had,
The boy must go and the girl must stay; that boy was a likely lad,
Would have been nineteen if he'd lived, might be earning a good sum now,
For Willie was something like me, wide awake, had a sensible brow;
But Ethel, poor child, her mother again lives in a world of her own,
Sees faces in flowers, hears voices in winds, reads poems from chiselled stone.
I certainly havn't had the best of luck, I've tried in different lands,
And, as I said, it's a drag to have others upon your hands.
'Twas a most disappointing thing, of course, when that old aunt died at Ayr,
And only one hundred pounds was left to Aimee, her rightful heir;
Not that I married Aimee for wealth, but I thought it just as sure,
That grand estate, to think of it all, and I lying here so poor.
Ah, I want some brandy! I must have something to make me feel more

strong.
Brandy! it is money, and life, and health; what makes Aimee stay so long?
Oh, here you are, make up more fire; I should think you're warm enough
Walking about, let me have that shawl, to-night will be wild and rough.
I must have some more spirit to keep me up, not that I heed the lie,
The doctor told you this morning that before very long I must die.
I expect, if I had some of the gold your old aunt used to keep,
He would manage to raise me up all right--you think I had better sleep,
You think me ungrateful, perhaps; reach some brandy and then you'll see
How more than grateful I am, what a pattern of patience I'll be.
No money, no means, the last thing's gone, and Ethel and you in need!
Well, you must have managed badly enough with only two mouths to feed,
For you can't count me as much, the little support I take,
A little stimulant now and then, swallowed only for your sake.
Aimee, I must have some now--nothing left? what is that glittering thing?
Aimee, you dear one, dispose of that; of what use is our wedding ring?
Don't be cross for the sake of the child, you say, why you angel dear,
Who would ever doubt you, so good, so true, you have nothing to fear.
And then you're always trusting in God, and surely he would approve
Of your selling your wedding ring for him that you've sworn to love?
I wish that wind would stop howling, it says such queer things to me,
Wake up, little Ethel, and send her before it's too dark to see
If that old fraud of a pawnbroker gives her the change all right.
Aimee, send quickly, I feel so strange; oh, I dread this coming night.
I never murdered that man out there, away on the western plains;
And yet there are spots of blood on the floor, they can't wash out the stains.
What is it the lawyers call it? "Accessory to the fact?"
Ha! ha! old boy, I was wide awake; they could not catch me in the act,
So we put that poor young fool of a lad, just out from the motherland,
Made him just drunk enough to fight when we needed a helping hand;
A helping hand with a bowie knife and a corpse to be stowed away,
We were sober enough not to be on hand when called upon next day.
Who's that? Who are you? Stop! stop! coming whispering into my ear,
"There are other judges, other law courts, and I have cause to fear."
How the ship struggles and reels--all right--is this the Australian shore?
No, sandbars and reefs; will they never stop those confounded breaker's roar?
Aimee, what is it? Take that stuff? I will if 'twill make me sleep.
I cannot rest; shall I never be quiet; hark how the wild winds sweep.
No, Victor, no; you got the money, and that was enough for you.
Did you think I was fool enough, man, to let you have Aimee too?
Aimee, come here and whisper to me; what does the judgment mean?
Judgment and conscience.--Look, look, there's Victor grinning behind the

screen!
Victor in heaven this many a year? I tell you it is no such thing.
Aimee, you were dead once--were drowned--did you hear the mermaids sing?
I say you were drowned one night, when the pleasure boat struck the bar,
And before any help could come you had floated out deep and far.
Every available thing was done that sailor or landsman could try;
But you could not be found--I guess not--so of course you had to die.
Hav'nt I a remarkable memory? these were the words I wrote:
"Every available thing was done by sailor or landsman afloat."
So Victor knows all about it--there! there he is coming again;
No! no! we are'nt here, we're away on the southern Indian main.
Who calls me? Who wants me? I cannot go into that wild dark land.
Somebody, help! Is this death? Don't touch me with that cold hand.
Aimee, don't leave me; oh say, have the officers found me at last?
Tell me--I think it's the medicine I took that makes me dream of the past--
Oh, will they believe me up there, in the clear bright rays of the sun,
That shows all the by-gone years of a life, the crimes a man has done?
Will nobody stop that horrid wind? it creeps right into my heart,
It seems to mutter, and groan and shriek: "Come, it is time to depart."
There's a broad dark sea before me; help, Aimee, the waters are deep!
I want a pilot--I cannot steer--I am sinking--let--me--sleep."

Bloweth the storm more cheerlessly still,
And the setting sun has a sickly hue,
As if he foresaw the falling tears,
As if all the sorrows of earth he knew.

Heavily stealeth an hour or two,
And mid the noise of the city's din,
No one noticed the tenement room
"As two passed out where but one went in."

For, lieth a dead man behind the door,
Closed between him and the outer strife,
And a weeping woman and clinging girl
Look upon death, and look out upon life.

Almost fainting with suffering and grief;
Alone, unknown, in a stranger land,
Mother and daughter have knelt to pray
As men pray wrecked on a rocky strand.

Churlishly gloweth the charcoal flame,
Mother and child with hearts almost broke,
Clasped in each other's embrace of love,
Checking her sorrow, sweet Ethel spoke:

"Mother, my mother dear,
Weep not so hopelessly, though all is dark
We have our loving Father yet in heaven,
His eyes must be upon our shattered bark;
Our sails are torn and we are tempest driven,
    Yet *He* can hear.

    To whom has God sent aid?
To the lone widow's home the prophet came,
For a few frightened men the wild sea slept,
For one poor servant flashed the glowing flame,
Where angels in their martial glory stepped
    Out from the shade.

    Not for proud Miriam's king
Rolled back the billows of the deep Red sea;
For helpless women, children, unarmed men,
The 'Fourth Man' walked to shield the flame-girt three;
For one, St. Michael, paced the lion's den,
    God's help to bring.

    Mother, is He not near,
Who had not where to rest His tired head?
Who, in the dreary wilderness alone,
Hungry and faint, had none to give Him bread;
Listening t' the damp wind's low and sullen moan
    O'er nature's bier."

"My child, my comforter, in this dark hour of love
Thy faith and trust in God is like the pole star's glow
To some benighted sailor; yes, e'en now a thought
Has come to me like light from dawning sunbeam brought.
My father, Ethel, was a Mason; ere he died
He called me to him, and kneeling at his side,
Gave me a jewel, charged me with his dying breath
Never to give it up except for life or death,
For when at last he died we were almost alone,
And stranger's ears were those which heard his dying moan,
The hands of strangers robed him for the grave,
The feet of strangers laid him where the cedars wave.
Weary, he had left England for the balmy breath
Of summer climes he found fierce pain and death.
I was his joy, his all on earth, for the dark hour
That gave me breath took home his purest flower.
And I have never known what means that place of rest,

The sweeetest home on earth, a living mother's breast.
All the night long, in which my father died,
He kept me close beside him, oft he vainly tried
To tell me about something, ever and anon
He'd speak about his brothers--I knew he had none--
Then in faint accents he would say, 'When I am cold
Tell them I left a lamb outside the fold.'
'Tell whom?' I cried. 'My brothers.' Then he'd fall asleep,
And I supposed him wandering and would weep.
A year or so before we spent a happy time
On bonnie Scotland's hills of heather and wild thyme,
And oft we watched the shepherd tending flocks of sheep
In the soft grassy vales, or up the mountain steep,
And sweet were the life lessons that I often took
From that unsullied page of nature's open book.
There came to me through that fair, hallowed summer scene,
Bright glowing visions of the fadeless pastures green,
And clearer views of One I trust my soul will keep,
That sinless, Holy Shepherd of the helpless sheep.
And so I thought when father moaned amid his pain,
'I leave an orphan lamb;' he had gone back again
Through the fierce fevers, annihilating flight,
To valley of the blue bell, or the heath crowned height.
But, suddenly there came one quick and conscious gleam
Of light with its belongings; that transforming beam
Lit up the past a moment, then its God-sent light
Flashed up the path he travelled. No more tears, no night
Was there for him, he said, only love is shining day,
And calling on his young wife's name he passed away.
Ethel, I've been so hungry often, and so chill,
And what is ten times worse, have seen you faint and ill,
And never yet have I foresworn my pledge; but now
Our duty to the dead must plead my broken vow.
Ethel, if my loved Father is with us to-night,
Will he not stamp forgiveness on this dead as right?
Perhaps in the morning light this howling storm will stay
Its fury, and God please to open up our way.
So we can lay our dead in quiet rest at last,
Then we, my child, go forth and dare the world's cold blast."

    "Mother, oh let me tell
Something I saw to-day: I went for bread;
But when I came to pass the church, my way
Was stopped by a procession, a neighbor said

It was St. John's loved Festival, a day
    Masons keep well.

    And while we were delayed
She spoke of one who had kind words for all,
She said his name was Roy, told me his home;
He could'nt have heard her, yet he looked at me
So strangely, yet so kindly, that my thoughts will roam
    To him for aid.

    Yes, mother; yes, to-night,
Trust me with that Masonic jewel, I
Will keep it safe; perhaps this very man
May know of some one who would like to buy,
At least he'll let me know its worth, I can
    But do the right.

    Mother, deny me not,
I'll go as "Esther went unto the king,
God will protect me if the night is wild;
Perhaps some bright ray of sunshine I may bring,
Pray that good angels may surround your child,
    And guard her lot."

Ethel's Mission.

Out in the blinding and pitiless sleet,
  The young girl goes on her errand blest;
She starts at each sound on the lonely street,
  As she longs for, but dares not dream of rest.

She knows not the worth of the gem she holds
  Close to her breast, in her thinly clad hands;
A martyr's courage her soul enfolds,
  And a guardian angel near her stands.

She shudders oft as she passes by
  Some staggering form, whose ribald curse
Seems, 'mid the storms of that stormy sky,
  To make the loneliness ten times worse.

Now on the icy pavement she stands,
  Now is plunged deep in a drift of snow,
Now she is rubbing her freezing hands
  Scarcely knowing which way she must go.

She thinks of the past, the long dark past,
  And blights that follow a drunkard's child,
And the tears she strive's to check fall fast,
  And turn to ice in that night so wild.

For we all know how, in the darkest shade,
  Dreams of the sunniest light will come
To one in a foreign hospital laid,
  No words so dear as, "My home, sweet home!"

And Ethel sees visions of sunny bowers
  Where once she played with the ring-doves mild,
'Mid the piercing blast she can scent the flowers
  She plucked with joy when a little child.

Then she starts in fear, and a nameless dread,
  As she thinks of her mother o'er and o'er,
Keeping lone watch with one lying dead,
  In that fearful stillness, behind the door;.

And, raising her trembling heart to Heaven,
  She asks of Him, who careth for birds,
That help and strength may to her be given,
  And not in air die her earnest words.

She reaches the end of the lonely gloom,
  She scarcely knows if in fear or joy,
She passes on to a snug warm room
  And stands in the presence of Victor Roy.

With tremulous efforts the timid girl
  Strives to utter her story of grief,
all things grow of a dizzy whirl
  As she shivering stands like an aspen leaf.

He looks at the eyes so earnest and sad,
  He hears the voice that is sweet and mild,
He sees a figure scantily clad,
  And only mutters, "Why, that is the child."

He looks at the snowflakes melting fast
  From the faded hood and the mantle fold,
While his thoughts go dreamily into the past,
  And now he is young and now he is old.

He has taken the jewel in his hand,
  He knows the mark which that Key-stone bears;
Upon any sea, upon any land,
  The sign of a brother that jewel wears.

He looks at the Key-stone, with eyes whose ray
  Grows dreamy like a somnambulist,
and Ethel murmurs, "I saw you to-day
  At the church of St. John, the Evangelist.

Have I done any wrong in coming here?
  'Twas only this evening my father died,
And mother is lonely and full of fear;
  We have no friend in this world so wide."

And hearing the mournful voice again,
  Seemed the unexplained spell to break;
And, in tones which were partly born of pain
  And partly of hopefulness, Victor spake:

"Come nearer the fire, little girl, and tell me why here you came.
Why did you bring this jewel to me? How did you learn my name?
Your father is dead, this was not his; your name is Ethel Adair.
Adair, Adair, it seems like a dream; I have heard that name, but where?
There, rest yourself child, it's cold to-night, you can tell me by and by
Where you are from, and where you live--what do you say, will I buy?
Do not fear little girl, I am your friend; you cannot speak the word

Of thanks you wish to say, never mind, for there's One above has heard.
Were you born in America? No; in Spain by the Darro's waters bright,
Your parents went there from western skies, 'neath the Rocky mountain's height.
Where do you live? What there, in that wretched barn of a place!
A man who can rent such dens should meet the contempt of his race.
What have you had to eat to-day? Why, how have you lived it out?
Your mother and you did sewing; oh yes, at starvation prices, no doubt.
Him? I know the man you have worked for then, he keeps his carriage and pair,
Gives largely to missionary funds, and is long and loud in grayer.
Never mind, the same All-Seeing Eye watches them come and go,
That noted the whited sepulchre two thousand years ago.
There, take that coffee and cake, and when you are rested I'll come
And see what has to be done in your lonely, desolate home.
And Jasper, you'll come along to take care of us both, and please bring
Something to eat; a basket? yes, filled with every good thing.
There, don't be long Jasper, time flies; yes, I know it is growing late,
And Una and her lion have not so very long to wait.
You used to read of Una, and wonder what made the lion stay;
Lions are useful, Ethel, sometimes to keep the jackals away.
Why child, are you ready so soon? Will you be my little guide?
Oh, I cannot tell you the worth of this; do you know where your grandpa died?
You would rather I bought it--all right--who is at home, only your mother, dear?
A brother's daughter and orphan child must not perish while I am near.
You knew that God would help you, have you learnt to trust and love Him too?
There's another link between us then, ever old and ever new.
You're afraid the storm will hurt me, you are used to the frosty air;
We'll brave it together for once, so come little Ethel Adair.

Aimee's Soliloquy.

And has she gone--that fair, frail, gentle flower--
Out in this scene of winter's frost-forged power?
Oh, heaven, have I been selfish in my woe?
Sweet angels guard her through the blinding snow.
Ethel, my child, my comforter, my stay,
It seems a long dream since the summer day
When first she came to me, in that far land
Where the bright Darro laves the gleaming sand.
'Neath the blue skies of Spain her baby feet
First walked amid the southern bowers, sweet
With breath of jasemine; and the green vines twined
Their gentle arms, clasping the golden rind
Of ripened oranges, and the rose-hung bowers
Glowed with the glory of a thousand flowers.
And oft at night, up the dark waters came
The splash of oars, beneath the stars white flame
Sounded the solemn chant of sailors nigh,
"Ave Maria! save us, hear our cry."
But to my babe and I there came no hymn,
No hallowing words amid the olives dim,
Only the same dark blight on every scene,
The leper's mournful cry, "Unclean, unclean."
For then 'twas whispered that dark deeds of shame
Wreathed with a viper's slime our household name.
I know not all the truth, but I am sure
The path of sin is downward, and the poor
Weak soul that yields is bound by fetters tight
'Till comes the end as it has come to-night.
And he lies there; oh, in this bitter cup
Which Thou, my Father, bids't me drink up.
I bless thy strong, calm power, which, through the years,
The long, dark, downward time of change and tears
Hast kept before my dimmed and fading sight
One word which warned with an undying light,
When love had proved an "*ignis fatuus*" gleam.
Duty stood forward with a godlike beam,
And brought before the fainting sickened heart,
The words God listened to, "till death us part,"
Two short words, Love and Duty, when together
How bearable the rains of stormy weather;
But when they unclasp hands, e'en then the dew

Grows into ice-points, piercing through and through.
"Till death us part," and am I really free?
Is the chain severed for eternity?
Look back my conscience, for the hours go fast,
Through the dim corridors of the far past.
Oh memory, from what point will thou start,
Back to the time when Victor won my heart;
He was my idol, bright star of my life,
Our home was planned, I was to be his wife;
When off to India he sailed far away,
Expecting to return an early day.
Ah, that last night when he put out to sea,
When by his side I sang "Abide with me;"
Ah, mournful days, yet hopes bright fires would burn,
Giving warm promise of his quick return,
Oft would I stand beside the untiring seas,
And send him words of love and trust like these:

"Evening's gloom is round me now,
Evening's breeze is whispering low,
Gentle murmuring voices wake
From the ripples of the lake.
Maker of the land and sea,
Hear my humble evening plea,
Father, hear me as I pray,
One I love is far away.

Guide the bark that bears him on,
Up the mountain's towering height,
And the misty damps of night,
In the city's moving throng,
With the wood-dove's sweetest song,
By the lonely river's marge,
O'er him give Thy angels charge.

In his hours of gladsome mirth,
Round some warm and welcome hearth,
In the halls of keen debate,
And the pomp and pride of state,
Cheer his spirit with love's beams
Lighten up his midnight dreams;
In his wanderings free and wild,
Father, keep him, as Thy child.

  From the pestilential blight,
  From the sun-beams scorching light,
  From temptation's mighty power,
  In some lone unguarded hour.
  From the dangers that we know,
  From the dark undreamt of foe,
  From the death-splash of the wave,
  Father, hear and help and save."

Then came the tidings brought by Robert's hand,
Victor lay buried in a far off land;
Died, wafting my name up to Heaven in prayer,
Leaving his promised bride to Robert's care.
Oft it has puzzled me, until my brain
Has racked itself from thinking into pain,
Why Victor left me thus, for in the past
He surely loved not Robert, perhaps at last
He saw things differently and thought it best
And had his wishes writ, e're he could rest.
But oh, the agony of those past hours;
It seems on looking back, that all my flowers
Looked mournfully at me and drooped their heads,
And lay like dying children in their beds;
And the bright birds in the vine-covered wall
Sang the sad chords of "The Dead March in Saul;"
And I was living, but all else were dead,
The sunbeam shimmered sickly o'er my head,
As when a ray peers in a darkened room,
Where one beneath a pall awaits his tomb.
Robert was ever near when Victor died,
And soon he sought to win me for his bride;
He told me how he'd loved me many years,
Loved him I loved, kindly he dried my tears,
Pictured my desolate and lonely lot,
Urged me to go with him to some new spot
Where all the past should be but as a dream,
And our lives glide gently down life's stream.
I told him that my heart was far away,
Beneath the palm where Victor's body lay;
That nightly in my dreams I heard the splash
Upon the shores where Ganges' waters dash.
I told him all my hope now was to stand
Amid the quiet of God's summerland;
Beneath another palm tree's shade to be,

And list the murmurs of the crystal sea.
But Robert loved me; I became his wife;
Could I forsee the sunken rocks of life?
And he was handsome then, and kind, and bright;
Could I foretell eclipses? then the night.
Oh, I have looked sometimes upon that face,
When robbed of every lineament of grace,
And I have cried unto the heavens above,
"It was not this, O God, I pledged to love;
Unsteady gait, wild brain and selfish heart--"
Flashed the red lights of danger "till death part."
Tell me, soul-searching ray, if erst I strove
To cherish, feed and guard where grew no love.
We sailed away to far Australia's shore,
Oh, the long days passed near the ocean's roar.
For him on whom I leaned in hope and trust,
Proved but coarse clay that crumbled soon to dust.
Drinking and gambling, sharks that swallow whole,
Homes, jewels, money, reason, body, soul.
Alone, for weeks to hear none call my name,
And happier alone; then baby came,
My firstborn, precious boy, I lived for him
For months; then his bright eyes grew dim,
And where the reeds and grass grew rank and wild,
We made a grave for Willie, darling child.
Ah, well I ween the night we laid him there,
I went to watch his grave; day had been fair,
But eve came up with thunder's muttered growl,
And ever and anon the lightning's scowl
Flashed angrily upon me as I viewed
The breakers dashing on the sea beach rude.
I grew passionate amid the whirlwind's sigh,
It had no word of comfort, loud was its cry,
And deep, dark was the struggle of my soul,
As I watched the billows onward roll.
There came no ray of hope across my breast,
As I turned toward my place of wild unrest;
I looked in vain for calmness, up on high,
It was not God's time for rainbows in the sky.
I went again next eve; there was no storm,
The full moon lighted up each darkening form;
'Twas the glory of a summer's bloom,
And I went onward to my baby's tomb.

I laid fresh flowers above the cold in death,
I felt upon my cheek warm zephyr's breath,
It seemed as if an angel had swept by
Across the grass where I too longed to lie;
And I saw the glorious sweep of moonbeams
Gilding the white rocks, circling all the streams
With rays of glory; I knelt on the bank,
Watching the picture, till my lone heart sank
Down to the depths; I could have slept to death,
My wounds seemed to defy the balmy breath
Of nature to restore my peace; my hands
I stretched out o'er the sea to northern lands,
I moved so swiftly o'er the moon gilt foam,
I stood once more within my father's home,
Could almost hear the village bells ring out,
Could almost hear the merry children's shout,
Could breathe the scent of violet and rose,
Walked down the dells where the pale primrose grows.
Ah, tell the truth, felt once again the bliss
Of Victor's loving clasp and burning kiss,
Felt his fond arms enfold me to his breast,
And I a bird safe in its shadowy nest,
And then the vision vanished; I was there,
A prey to sorrow, loneliness and care,
Like one who spends in a dark mine his life,
My baby dead, and I a drunkard's wife.
Then came a thought on Him of Mary born,
Who turned not back for spear or cross or thorn,
And through the murmurings of breeze and bay,
A voice seemed whispering to me, "Watch and pray."
I knelt as He knelt on the grassy sod,
And following Him I prayed for strength from God;
A sweet bird suddenly broke into song,
A soft air trembled through the branches strong,
And my soul rose on the pure air to Heaven,
Thus to my heart was hope and comfort given.
While by that grave I sang "Abide with me,"
As on the night when Victor went to sea;
Ah, I was leaning then upon the breast
That five-and-twenty years has been at rest.
Oh, Victor! art thou gone so far away
That thou cans't hear no earth tone night or day?
Sometimes it seems as if thou wert not far,

Nearer and warmer than the nearest star.
How the wind moans--Ethel, my precious one,
Where shall we wander by to-morrow's sun?
Homeless and friendless in a stranger land,
Our Saviour help and aid; Thy mighty hand
Can save, Thine ear can list each bitter moan.
Hark! Ethel's voice, she comes, and not alone!

Twelve Month's After.

Still rolleth onward time's mystical tide,
  Ebbing and flowing by night and day;
Gladness and misery scattering wide,
  Gladness and misery turning away.

Fair Spring has been with her emerald leaves,
  Red Summer with roses of crimson ray,
Brown Autumn has passed with its golden sheaves,
  Again St. John the Evangelist's day.

Since the morning came, Masonic bands
  Have gathered, old friendship's ties to renew;
True hands have been clasped in a brother's hands,
  Calm rest and refreshment fall like dew.

Far over the roll of the billowy seas,
  Strangers have met on the lodge-room floor,
And like Israel encamped beneath Elim's trees,
  Have thirsted for love's cool draught no more.

From the ice-wrought chain of the Arctic zone,
  To the silver-lit sands of rich Peru;
From the shores which guard Victoria's throne,
  To the woods of the west, unshorn and new.

In the crowded street, full of noise and cheer,
  In hamlets and villages, still and calm;
Where the northern bear glides cold and clear,
  Or the southern cross tints the sacred palm.

Over the face of this wonderful earth,
  Templars haye met in Encampment dear,
Prisoners of hope have changed sighing for rest,
  Pilgrims have tarried where angels were near.

Souls that were longing for far better things,
  Their faith growing dulled by the Siroc's blight,
Have shaken the dust from their weary wings,
  And plumed them again for a higher flight.

They have spoke of the work of the by-gone year,
  Of Ashlers now perfected true and square,
Of weary hands folded upon the bier,
  Of souls passed on to a lodge room fair.

They have told of storms from the North, so chill,
  How dark was the South when the daylight ceased;
They have watched the sun neath the Western hill,
  They have hailed his light in the holy East.

They have sang of the victor knights whose swords,
  Are sharpened to slay the dark hosts of sin;
Still marching on through Saracen hordes,
  Till the King's Encampment at last they win.

They have knelt in prayer round the altar's shade,
  And implored what man never asks in vain,
That creation's Grand Architect will aid,
  The builders to build till calm rest they gain.

Brave hearts have brightened love's armor anew,
  And so shall the magical spell last on,
Till all who have worked by his pattern true,
  Shall meet face to face their beloved St. John.

Within the dwelling of Victor Roy,
  A fair girl awakens soft music's power,
And a woman listens in silent joy,
  To the thrilling strains at that quiet hour.

"Ethel, my child, cease playing, come to me,
There, lean your head upon your mother's knee,
Do you remember dear what night this is?
Look back at last St. John's day, then at this,
You've often wondered why upon that night,
When you my guide led from the gloom to light;
That when you gave the name Adair it seemed,
To him who heard it, as if he had dreamed.
Like a dim funeral knell from some old chime,
Heard years ago, in some far distant clime,
Ethel, we should speak kindly of the dead,
Unable to defend themselves, their spirits fled
To worlds unknown to us, we cannot see
The homes they occupy, the destiny
It pleases God to give them, this we know
That our reaping must be what we sow,
If we plant thistles, we the thorn shall meet,
If we sow ripe grains, we shall harvest wheat,
And something else we know of future life,
That be the memories of war and strife,
Of evil thoughts which may have been controlled

Of hearts through which wild passions unchecked rolled;
Of base mean deeds that burn like felon brand,
In the pure sunlight of the eternal land;
Or if sweet recollections of the past,
Of homes where love her golden radiance cast,
Of deeds of mercy unto man unknown,
But breathing incense to the star-gemmed throne;
We know that not one of Adamic race,
Is unknown unto Him, the Lord of Grace,
And with the thoughts that shape themselves to prayer,
We can but leave them in His gracious care,
Who, as sharp nails were piercing each vein through,
Prayed 'Father forgive, they know not what they do,'
And preached of mercy to the souls in prison,
Ere He from the well guarded tomb had risen;
So darling think as gently as you may,
On one you saw so sadly pass away.
But duty bids me tell you, deeds of shame,
Stamped dark dishonor on our household name,
When we were living in the distant west,
A trouble came; grief was no stranger guest,
For racking fears sad day and anxious night,
Seemed to hold life-long leases as their right,
The trouble came through some high words at play.
All I know was before noon next day,
A letter came bidding me leave that night;
Bring what I could and let none know my flight,
To change my name, and if need be to swear
I never knew 'Montrose' only 'Adair.'
Part truth, part falsehood born of inward shame,
That sank the true one for the middle name,
I heard that dark red stains ended a strife
Began in so-called play, and closed with life.
I know for many months a nameless dread,
Hung like the sword of Damocles overhead,
And we again had crossed the stormy main
And hid away among the hills of Spain,
But when you were an infant, nurse and I
Took you one morning ere the sun was high,
And in the little church covered with vines,
O'er which the setting sun in glory shines,
We gave you into the good Shepherd's Care
Amid our falling tears and Heaven sent prayer;

And there without respect to friends or foes,
Stands your true name, Ethel Adair Montrose.
My child before you close your eyes to-night,
With no forebodings for to-morrow's light,
Return your heartfelt thanks to Him whose hand
Has led us safely through a desert land,
Has kept our feet on many a slippery way,
And guided us from midnight to the day,
Lay at the Glorious Giver's blessed feet,
All that he asks, your time that passes fleet,
Your heart's first holiest love, your talents give
To him who scorned not death, that we may live."

   Mother, I'll not forget,
To ask rich blessings upon you and him,
Whom God sent as a life boat to the lost,
A year ago to-night, when on the dim
Dark seas of woe, our bark was tempest toss'd,
   The sun of hope had set.

   I'm glad I went to-day,
And laid a cross upon that snow-strewn grave,
The sun gleamed out and on the white leaves burned,
It seems as if the childhood love, I gave
The one that calmly sleeps there, had returned
   Watch to keep o'er his clay.

   And yet it's not the same
In quality, the love I cherish now
Has more of pity perhaps; another one
Has surely right to my allegiance; how
Can I forget all he for us has done?
   Hark! now he calls my name.

Ethel! where are you, there is the group you were speaking about one day,
Do you know the faces, two you love best, then drive those tears away,
What is there to cry for child, in a locket that's new and bright,
It was to have been your Christmas gift, but it's just as good to-night,
It bears the name of the day you came to spoil my dog and cat,
My birds and me too I'm afraid, if you say much more like that.
Sing me something instead, it's scarcely supper time yet--my child;
I see you are weary, go and rest while these winter winds blow wild,
Ethel, before you say 'good night,' we will sing "Abide with me,"
As I heard it twenty-six years ago the night I went to sea.

And softly upon the evening air,
  The strain of praise from true hearts was given
And angels wafted the holy prayer,
  Like incense up to the throne of Heaven.

"Good night, sweet Ethel," a silence fell
  Solemn and calm, by no whisper broke,
Two sat watching the fire, a spell
  Seemed holding each, until Victor spoke.

"Of what are you thinking so earnestly, you fancy I know the thought,
That has grown to deep for utterance, with strange sad memories fraught,
A year, a memorable year ago, yes, we shall ne'er forget,
That day of St. John the Evangelist, that night when two old friends met,
'Twas a dreary watching too my love, all that night in solemn gloom,
Where the dead lay cold and silently, waiting his lonely tomb,
I am glad that Ethel went to-day, and laid a cross on that grave,
I am glad that we each can truly say at the judgement day, 'I forgave,'
I read some lines the other day, that may have been written for us,
Heart histories repeat themselves like others, the lines ran thus:

"And midnight wearily stole on,
  Heavy clouds o'er the young moon swept,
We looked out upon life and prayed
  We looked upon the dead and wept,
That God can work while man looks on,
  That truth will triumph o'er our dread,
A lesson sometimes hard to learn,
  We learnt while watching by the dead.

'Twas not a scene that lovers choose,
  Did any say that we had loved,
The dead was by us, yet we knew,
  That we were living and beloved,
Truth's talisman was on each heart
  Oh, was there sin in what we said,
The troubles told, the truth confessed,
  The night we watched beside the dead."

Aimee, look at this jewel rich, I have worn it the live long day,
You think I value it, so I do, yet I deem it worthless clay,
Compared with the other jewel rare, this Keystone brought to me,
Bright gem, long hidden but not destroyed in some unfathomed sea,
More honorable than golden fleece, more precious than the stone,
That alchemysts seek vainly for, or gems of a regal crown,
A Keystone brought to light once more, all uninjured by the storm,

The rains of fire that have swept round my other jewel's form,
For the fire doth but clear the dross, the waves but wash the dust,
From off the jewels of purest gold, such jewels I hold in trust,
For I should have claimed you still as mine, if we never more had met,
Till free from stain of sorrow or sin we stand where hope's suns ne'er set,
Where angels live on, in their life of love, unchanged yet ever new,
And then the time, God's own right time would have come for my taking you,
For this re-union upon earth, is the sign, beloved wife
Of the eternal rest we'll share in the bright hereafter life;
For have we not assurance blest, that whichever first goes home,
Will await with loving patience, till the other one shall come,

Unto those who wear God's blessed seal upon each united heart,
Those words must half their horror lose 'until death do you part,'
For true love doth dissolve death's power, as spring's suns melt the snow,
'Tis the only password at the gates, through which we both must go,
Where born of that benevolence which fills our Father's breast,
Angelic masons now prepare our special house of rest,
God's promises will never fail, if we but wait His hours,
He sends His messages of peace, like His rainbow after showers,
O'er one beam of that holy arch, this scroll now seems to glide,
"After the dark and dreary day, it shall be light at eventide."

Miscellaneous Pieces

Mist and Sunshine.

I looked, and the mist had hidden
  Streamlet and gorge and mountain,
Mansion and church had vanished away,
  No trace of tree or fountain.
Mist, on the roof where birdlings wake
  The strains of old love stories,
Mist, like tears on the roses' cheek,
  In cups of the morning glories.

"Ah, like life, 'said my heart to me,'
  Only a world of sorrow,
The lips you love, the hands you clasp,
  Are cold and strange to-morrow.
Mists on the stream of by-gone days,
  Where are your childhood bowers?
Mists on the path of coming years.
  Where are your household flowers?"

I looked again; a sunbeam bright
  Had shot through the heavy mist;
It drew the rose to its glowing breast,
  And the morning glories kissed.
The spire of the Ascension Church
  Flashed out like St. 'Michael's sword,
When girt with glowing armor, he
  Doeth battle for his Lord.

Each moment some high roof or tower,
  Some flush of the maple leaves,
Grew fair to sight, the birdlings sang
  In nests on the sun-lit eaves;
And Nature bathed in living light,
  As if she renewed her birth,
The Universal Father smiled
  Through his sunbeam, on the earth.

"Ah, now my heart, so sad and cold
  With mists of its repining,
What will thou say to see once more

   The cloud with silver lining?"
Source of light! when I leave this sphere,
   Grant me a vision like this,
Mists and shadows rolling away
   From the Paradise of bliss.

May I look thus on mounts of God,
   The flash of temple spires,
And hear the deathless singers chant
   From their harmonious lyres;
So may I close mine eyes on earth,
   While heaven's pure light is breaking,
And some I know will fold me close,
   In arms of love awaking.

Charge to the Knight of Malta

Air--Stephenos

Lo, a knight in armour standing,
  Ready for the foe;
Thee we greet, belov'd Companion,
  Thee we know.

Keep thine oath, oh new made soldier,
  Pledged in heaven's sight;
Nor forget the vow thou'st taken,
  Malta's knight.

By the banner, o'er us waving,
  By thy lance at rest,
Chiefly by that Cross emblazoned
  On thy breast.

In the heat of danger's trial,
  Dare the fiercest fight;
No desertion, no denial,
  Right or life!

See thou turn not from the conflict,
  On the battle field,
Though men bear a dying soldier
  On thy shield.

Let thy strong arm shield the helpless,
  And the feeble save;
Mercy's voice the true knight knoweth,
  And the brave.

Welcome, dear Sir Knight, thrice welcome!
  To our tented field;
God will aid us till the final
  Foe shall yield.

We are pledged unto His kingdom,
  Who for us hath borne
Cross and spear, for us did suffer
  Crown of thorn.

Then, for Him who rose triumphant
  To the heavenly Lamp,
Gird thy sword though night surround thee,
  Wild and damp.

When at last, in mortal weakness,
  Sword and spear must fall,
Christ, unto Thy Grand Encampment,
  Take us all.

The Curl of Gold.

How wildly blows the wintry wind, deep lies the drifting snow
On the hillside, and the roadside, and the valleys down below;
And up the gorge all through last night the rushing storm flew fast,
And there old walls and casements were rattling in the blast.
Lady, I had a dream last night, born of the storm and pain,
I dreamed it was the time of spring; but the clouds were black with rain.
I thought that I was on the bay, a good way out from shore
Alone, and feeling much afraid at the wild tempest's roar,
I tried to reach the distant land, but could not find the way,
And suddenly my boat capsized far out upon the bay.
I shrieked in wildest agony amid the thunder shock,
When I heard you saying unto me, "Beneath us is a Rock,
Trust not to me, these waves are strong, but lift your tear-dimmed eye--
That star will lead us to the rock that higher is than I."
And through the drenching wave and surf, together on we passed,
Till the bright green slopes of Hamilton shone clearly out at last.
It seemed so strange, we stepped ashore, your garments were all dry,
And, holding hands as we do now, I heard you say "good-bye."
Dear lady, now I see it all, those blessed words you said
Were with me in the storm last night, like angels round my bed.
"So many and great dangers that we cannot stand upright,"
"Defend us by thy mercy, from all perils of this night."
Lady, I am a mother, none know it here save you;
Don't blush for me, there is no shame, I am a wife, leal and true.
Lady, true love is born of heaven, we may deem it dead and past,
And sit with bowed down head alone, the heart's door closed and fast;
When suddenly we hear a voice, and spite of bolt or bar,
Like its dear Master, there it stands, stretching its arms afar;
Though buried up it rises, though dead it lives anew,
And breathes again its Master's words, "Sweet peace be unto you,"
Folks say, "There is a mystery about that poor sick girl,"
Lady, there's mystery round us all, that angels will unfurl,
I have one favor now to ask, within this paper's fold,
There's a little lock of baby's hair, just half one curl of gold,
When I am in my coffin, and soon now I'll be at rest,
Will you lay this little curl of gold upon my quiet breast,
God and the angels only know where the other half lies hid,
In the green sod of old Ireland, neath a baby's coffin lid,
Don't'leave me yet, it is near night, I feel so strange to-day,
You know the prayers for dying ones, oh kneel once more and pray,

Thank God for sending one to me, where the wild tempests roll,
You won't forget--the little curl--Saviour receive my soul.

Holy Communion.

We were wearied in the battle,
  Tempted, and pained, and tried
By day the din and the carnage,
  By night the rain's fierce tide;
But we heard a loving message,
  From the Prince's tent it came,
"Each meet in the banqueting house.
  In memory of my name."

We gathered; a motley regiment,
  Some young in the war of life,
Some chiefs in the Royal Army,
  Some old and sick with strife,
Some limped in the sacred pathway,
  Some were foot sore and worn,
Some had their lances all shivered,
  Some had their banners torn.

And we all looked dim and dusty;
  We all were stained with sin;
But we held the Prince's message,
  And the porter said "Come in."
We went to the banqueting house;
  We sat at the Prince's board,
There we polished each his helmet,
  We sharpened each his sword.

Our Prince--we talked of his strife,
  The forlorn hope He had led,
How He opened the gates of life,
  And rescued from Death the dead;
And with Him we saw a bright host,
  Our comrades gone on before,
The right wing of our army
  Upon the farther shore.

And the festering wound was healed.
  The banners were made whole,
Mists rolled back from the almost blind,
  Faith lit each warrior's soul;
We drank of the fruit of the vine,
  We ate the living bread,

The holy benediction fell,
  With healing on each head.

We entered in poor worn soldiers,
  We came out bolder knights,
To march on to the Prince's battle,
  And war for His glorious rights,
For had we not each re-taken
  The oath of allegiance high,
And sworn round the Royal Standard
  To conquer, or to die.

Song of Azael.

I heard the voice of the Death Angel speak,
  As slowly he pass'd me by,
And I saw him throw snow on the crimson cheek,
  And darken the laughing eye.
I saw him glide down through many a street;
  Tears followed him like spring rain;
And yet ever unheeding tears or prayers,
  He mattered his wild wild refrain,
"Come away with me, sweet baby so bright,
I love the young flowers of the rosebud's hue,
What? mother would keep thee always in sight,
And see the sad tears in those eyes so blue.
  Come with me, little one.
All thorns and crosses for you are done,
Mother will meet thee where all is fair,
Grown to the height of the angels there.
  Quiet and deep,
  Be now thy sleep,
  Baby, so white.

For thou shalt travel where sorrow and strife
Never shall darken thy pathway again.
Azael must take home to the Lord of Life
The darlings He bought on the cross with pain.
  Ah! you smile, little one.
Pleasure and glory for you are won,
Near to the angels, you're not afraid
Of going with me far into the shade.
    The casket grows cold,
    The jewel I hold,
    For hearts of love.

Come along with me, thou trader in gold,
Many have turned from thy office to-day.
Thou hast no time to consider the claim
Of the wronged or helpless who crossed thy way.
  You shudder, trembling one.
Close up the ledger, business is done.
Let you stay till your vessel comes in?
I'll take you far from the market's din,
  And you'll have time,

    In that strange clime,
    To meditate.

For thou wilt awaken, I would not hold.
If I could, the past from memory's ken.
I fancy that other ledgers unfold,
Their pages for some of you business men;
  Rest to night, tired one.
Not half of your merchandise is done?
The steamers, the banks, the corn exchange?
No, Azael deals not in notes or change;
    He keeps no gold,
    In his fingers cold,
    He takes no bribe.

Come along with me, sweet lady so fair,
Who told thee I was so grim and so cold;
Know you that I covet that sunny hair,
And those delicate arms's caressing fold;
  Fear me not, gentle one.
What if the hymn and the task are done,
In my arms there is far calmer rest,
Then thou wilt find on thy lover's breast.
    Sleep, sleep for awhile,
    Then waken to smile,
    Ever and aye.

True life is progressive, my lady fair,
And thou wilt re-open those radiant eyes;
Think you that I have no burden of care,
Azael has to account for each prize.
  Banish doubt, gentle one.
Quicksands and pitfalls for thee are all done;
Human love may ere long deceive thee,
But Azael's love will never leave thee
    Till those earth-dim eyes
    Look on Paradise,
    Never to weep.

The song of Azael melted away,
  On the solemn midnight's bieath,
I thought of the talents, the oilless lamps--
  Oh, Azael, Angel of Death,
I know that ere long thou wilt come for me.
    Immanuel, Lord of life,

By Thy victory gained on the bitter cross,
   Save in that hour of strife.

Only a Story

Let me tell you a story, dear,
  Of someone I saw to-day,
Only a man with a pale worn face,
  And auburn locks grown gray,
One, I thought would never again,
  Come over my pathway here,
One, I still hope to meet forgiven,
  In a better brighter sphere.

Why did you start, he knew me, yes,
  A flush as of pain, or pride,
Pass'd swiftly o'er the pale stern face,
  And the high white forehead dyed,
I heard the roll of carriage wheels,
  Unthinkingly raised my eyes,
One glance flashed out beneatt thosee Brows,
  Like lightening across the skies.

Shudder not dear, 'tis he who grieves,
  Not I in my lonely life,
I have a calm bright future now,
  He? well, he has gold and strife,
They say that oft by the heaving lake,
  He wanders about alone,
Waves that dash on the sandy beach,
  Answer his throbbing heart's moan.

Once or twice has been heard a name
  As if wrung with torturous pain,
From lips to sacred silence sworn,
  Told only to storms and rain.
He leaves the light of gilded halls,
  To clasp in the midnight air,
Some flowers that faded years ago,
  One lock of a girl's dark hair.

Ask me not with those pleading eyes,
  If I dream about him yet;
Is anything colder to your touch,
  Than ashes with rain-drops wet?
What is harder to kindle up,
  Than lava grown black and cold,

That once from burning mountain's heart,
  In fiery grandeur rolled.

Pity him, pray for him, that is well,
  Married for jewels and gold,
Vipers crawl from the caskets bright,
  And they keep his fingers cold.
Only a flush of pain or pride,
  When to-day our glances met,
He in his gorgeous wealth arrayed,
  I, out in the cold and wet.

Hush; as we sow we surely reap,
  Yes, he has a wife and gold,
Broad lands, a mansion white and tall
  Like an iceberg grand and cold,
I? I've the blessings of the poor,
  Which fall like the gentle dew,
I've claims on mansions far away,
  I have life, and love, and *you*.

Daybreak.

Turn thy fair face to the breaking dawn,
Lily so white, that through all the dark,
Hast kept lone watch on the dewy lawn,
Deeming thy comrades grown cold and stark;
Soon shall the sunbeam, joyous and strong,
Dry the tears in thy stamens of gold--
Glinteth the day up merry and long,
  And the night grows old.

Turn thy fair face to Faith's rosy sky,
Soul so white that lone night hath kept
Sighing for spirits sin-bound that lie;
Wrong has ruled right, and the truth has slept;
The dawn shall show thee a host ere long,
Planting sweet roses abqve the mould;
The sun of righteousness beameth strong,
  And sin's night grows old.

Turn thine eyes to the burnished zone
From out of thy nest neath darkened eaves,
Oh bird, who hast mingled thy plaintive moan
With sobbing winds through quivering leaves;
From thy heart, by light which groweth strong,
Draw out the thorns that pierced on the world;
Glinteth the day up merry and long,
  And the night grows old.

Turn thy sad eyes to God's summerland,
Mourner, who waileth some love laid past,
Some bark that has anchored on foreign strand
And left her sailors free from the blast;
They are not here where the grass grows long,
They are not down in the red-brown mould;
Heaven's day is coming up fair and strong,
  And earth's night grows old.

The Wife's Watch.

Sleep on, my darling, sleep on,
I am keeping watch by your side,
I have drawn in the curtains close,
And banished the world outside;
Rest as the reaper may rest,
When the harvest work is done
Rest as the soldier may rest,
When the victor's work is won.

You smile in your happy sleep:
Are the children with you now?
Sweet baby Willie, so early called,
And Nellie with thoughtful brow,
And May, our loving daughter.
Ah, the skies grew dark, my love,
When the sunshine of her presence
Vanished to Heaven above.

While you're resting, my darling,
I dream of the shadowy hour,
When one of us looks the last
On the light of its household bower,
Then a sad sigh heaves my breast,
And tears from my eyelids burst,
As I ask of the future dim,
"Which shall be summoned first?"

Sometimes I pray in terror
That you may be first to go,
Never again to sorrow,
Or to feel one throb of woe,
Beyond the mists of the river,
Where mystic shadows weave,
I have no fears, my beloved,
In One we both believe.

But I, oh I so lonely,
Could I look as I look now,
If this was thy last long sleep,
The ice of death on thy brow;
In sight of the holy angels,
I offer my earnest plea,

I cry to my God and pray,
"If one goes first, take me."

Our lives have been happy dear,
I fancy the tears we shed,
By our lost children's coffins.
On faces white and dead,
Are counted as dew drops now,
On the flowers early sown
In the gardens of Paradise,
The Lord's, and still our own.

So we'll leave the future dim,
Take the sunshine as we go,
And when we come to the brink,
Where black waves ebb and flow,
We'll trust the voice which summons,
The love that has ever kept,
To fold in his arms one taken,
To lead by His hand one left.

Adoniram.

A Legend of the Temple.

  The dew was gone,
The morn was bright, the skies were fair,
The flowers smiled neath the sunbeams ray,
Tall cedars grew in beauty there.
As Adoniram took his way,
  To Lebanon.

  Praise his heart filled,
More than four hundred years had fled,
Since from stern Egypt marched the bands,
Whose sons, with Solomon at their head,
And Tyrian brethern's skilful hands,
  Prepare to build.

  He watched them there,
Round every block, and every stone,
Masonic implements were laid,
But around *one* were many thrown,
And yet it seemed already made,
  Tried, true and square.

  He wandering spake,
"Are not all from one mountain brought
As jewels for a diadem,
Why, have they at this one stone wrought,
Will not all see Jerusalem.
  One house to make?"

  The Widow's son
Smiled kindly in his brother's face,
And said "All are made ready here,
But not all fill the same high place,
The Corner stone this will be near,
  When toil is done."

  The listener bent,
His eyes on the unfinished stone,
And found himself a wiser man,
Through that rough child of mountains lone,
A ray of the Grand Master's plan,
  To him was sent.

   From Masonry,
That just man learnt that woes are thrown
Around God's children, pain and care,
But draw them near the corner stone,
With the Great Architect to share,
   Heaven's blazonry.

Songs in the Night.

"Where is God my Maker, Who giveth songs in the night."--Bible.

The hour of midnight had swept past,
  The city bell tolled three,
The moon had sank behind the clouds,
  No rustling in the tree.
All, all was silent as the grave,
  And memories of the tomb,
Had banished sweet sleep far away,
  All spoke of tears and gloom.

When suddenly upon the air.
  Rang out a sweet bird's song,
No feeble, weak, uncertain note,
  No plaint of grief or wrong,
No "Miserere Domine,"
  No "Dies Irea" sad,
But "Gloria in Excelsis" rang,
  In accents wild and glad.

How could he sing? a birdling caged,
  And in the dark alone,
And then methought that he had seen,
  Some vision from God's throne,
The little birdling's eyes were bright,
  While mine with tears were dim,
Had some bright watcher glided by,
  And spake in joy to him?

Then I remembered what Christ said,
  The God of love's dear Son,
"Not one of these small birds forgot
  Beneath the glorious sun."
They have no load of grief to bear,
  Of sin no dark, deep stain,
And yet in patience take their share
  Of storm, and frost and rain.

Oh, can it be unknown to us,
  Without one human word,
The universal Father soothes
  The death-bed of each bird;

"The whole creation groaneth," yet
  These pure things of the sky,
Are they not nearer to the gates
  Than mortals such as I?

Yet while I mused, it seemed some form,
  Ere yet I was aware,
Bent o'er my pillow, dried my tears,
  And turned to sing my prayer;
Some subtle presence unrevealed,
  Seemed to repeat the words,
"Fear not, for you are dearer far,
  Than many little birds."

I do not ask what seemed to speak;
  Whether the angel blest,
Who hath been my appointed guard
  In calm or wild unrest;
Or whether some sweet voice I love,
  But hushed to me a while,
Came down on gentle mission sent,
  To change for tears a smile.

It matters not; God knows faith's wings
  Droop sometimes in the dust,
And hands grow weak and lose their hold
  On Hope's firm anchor trust;
And so, while sending dew and rain,
  And glowing sunbeams bright.
God giveth unto those who hear,
  Songs in the darkest night.

In Memoriam.

   They are gone away,
No prayers could avail us to longer keep
The ships called out on the unknown deep,
We saw them sail off, some lingeringly,
Some suddenly summoned put out to sea;
They stepped aboard, and the planks were drawn in,
But their sweet, pale faces were free from sin;
As they turned to whisper one last good bye,
We sent after each one a bitter cry;
  We knew on that track,
  They would never come back,
  By night or day.

   Ah, we've closed dear eyes,
But God be thanked that they, one and all,
Had the heaven light touch them before the pall;
They saw the fair land that we could not see,
And one said, "Jesus is standing by me,"
And one, "The water of life I hear,"
And one, "There's no suffering nor sorrow here,"
One, "I have seen the city of countless charms,"
One, "'Neath me are the Everlasting Arms,"
   So we know it is best,
   They should be at rest,
   In God's paradise.

   Mary's Blessed Son,
Thou wilt not chide if thou see'st that low
Our harps are hanging on willow bough;
We would not murmur, we know it is well,
They are gone from the battle, the shot and shell,
And in our anguish we're not alone;
The Father knows all the grief we have known;
Oh God, who once heard the Christ's bitter cry,
Thou knowest what we feel when we see them die.
   Our light, has been hid
   By the coffin lid,
   And dark our noon.

   God hears our moan,
He knows how a stricken heart had said,
"Oh, number her not with the silent dead,

For if she stays watching the golden sea,
God help, for what will become of me?
The last rose out of my childhood's bower,
From my English garden, the last sweet flower;
Take me instead, for none call me mother."
The messenger said, "I take no other."
  So she went the road
  The others have trod,
  And I am alone.

  We shall meet again;
I fancy sometimes how they talk together,
Of the way they travelled, the stormy weather
That beat so hard on their pilgrim road,
Now changed for the city of their God;
I wonder if in their special home,
They keep choice rooms till their darlings come.
Saviour, who loves them, protect and guide me
Where they are waiting 'neath life's fadeless tree,
  Father and mother,
  And elder brother,
  And sisters twain.

A Song of the Flowers.

"Why are you weeping, ye gentle flowers?
Are ye not blest in your sunny bowers?
Have you startling dreams that make ye weep,
When waking up from your holy sleep?

"Ah, knowest thou not, we fold at night,
The tears earth drops from her eyelids bright,
Like a loving mother her griefs are born,
Lest her tender nurslings should die ere morn,
And the sweet dew falls in each open cup,
Till the eyes of morn are lifted up;
We unfold our leaves to the sun's bright face,
And close them up at the night's embrace.

Dost thou ask if grief comes creeping across,
From the poplar bough to the dark green moss?
No, round us the sunbeams smile and glow,
Round us the streamlets dance and flow,
And the zephyr comes with its gentle breeze,
To sigh out its life in the young green trees,
And then from the beds where the flowers grow,
Rises a melody soft and low.

And the glorious rose with her flushing face,
And the fuschia with her form of grace,
The balsam bright, and the lupin's crest,
That weaves a roof for the firefly's nest;
The myrtle clusters, and dahlia tall,
The jessamine fairest among them all;
And the tremulous lips of the lily's bell,
Join in the music we love so well."

"But startle ye not when the tempests blow?
Have you no dread of a wily foe?
Do you not tremble, when the serpents hiss
Mid leaves that the zephyr alone should kiss?

Lady, the bells of the fainting flowers
Close at the coming of thunder showers;
The branches and tendrils merrily dance
At the whirlwind's cry, and the lightning's glance.
We dread not to see the snake's back of gold?
Dart through the lilacs or marigold,

For fears that dwell in the human breast,
Find in the heart of flowers no rest.

We have no fears when we hear thee pass
Over the fold of the tangled grass,
We have no dread when we hear thee breathe
Over the flowers we love to wreathe,
Nor tremble when night falls from heaven above,
And nature is stillness and earth is love;
We steal from thy keeping when summer is o'er,
And wait thee where flowers can die no more."

The Cities of Old.

Cities and men, and nations, have passed by,
Like leaves upon an autumn's dreary sky;
Like chaff upon the ocean billow proud,
Like drops of rain on summer's fleecy cloud;
Like flowers of a wilderness,
Vanished into forgetfulness.

O! Nineveh, thou city of young Ashur's pride,
With thy strong towers, and thy bulwarks wide;
Ah! while upon thee splashed the Tigris' waters,
How little thought thy wealth-stored sons and daughters,
That Cyaxerses and his troops should wait
Three long years before thy massive gate;
Then Medes and Persians, by the torches' light,
Should ride triumphantly thy streets by night;
And from creation banish thee,
O! Nineveh. O! Nineveh.

And country of the pride of Mizriam's heart,
With pyramids that speak thy wealth and art,
Why is it that no minstrel comes, who sings
Of all the glory of thy shepherd kings?
Tyre, why are thy walls in ruins thus?
Why is thy name so seldom spoke by us?
Sidon, among the nations thou art fled,
Thy joy departed and thy glory dead;
Far gone ere all thy generations,
Fallen nations! Fallen nations!

And Babylon, with all thy thronging bands,
The glory of Chaldea's ancient lands;
Thy temple, where a numerous host was seen,
Thy gardens hung to please the Midian queen;
Where beauteous flowers smiled on their terrace beds,
Proud kings have passed through thee, and crowned heads;
And grandeur and magnificence could view
In thee a resting place--thy stores not few;
Why is it thou art all alone?
O! Babylon. O! Babylon.

And Greece, who shone in literature and might,
When Marathon's broad plains saw sword and fight;

Thy monumental ruins stand alone,
Decay has breathed upon thy sculptured stone
And desolation walks thy princely halls,
The green branch twines around thy olden walls;
And ye who stood the ten years' siege of Troy,
Time's fingers now your battlements annoy;
Why is it that thy glories cease?
O! Classic Greece. O! Classic Greece!

And thou, best city of olden time,
O! we might weep for thee, once chosen clime.
City, where Solomon his temple reared,
City, where gold and silver stores appeared;
City, where priest and prophet lowly knelt,
City, where God in mortal flesh once dwelt.
Titus, and Roman soldiers, laid thee low,
The music in thy streets has ceased to flow;
Yet wilt thou not return in joy once more,
And Lebanon give up her cedar store?
And vines and olives smile as now they smile,
Yet not upon the ruin of a holy pile;
Wilt thou Destruction's flood not stem?
Jerusalem! Jerusalem!

Cities and men, and nations, have gone by,
Like leaves upon an Autumn's dreary sky;
Like chaff upon the ocean billow proud,
Like drops upon the summer's passing cloud;
Like flowers of a wilderness,
Vanished into forgetfulness.

Out of His Time.

One evening a short time since, our attention was attracted by the prolonged ringing of a bell. The given number of strokes had sounded, yet ring, ring, ring. Was it an alarm of fire? No other bell signalled an answer. Was it some danger to our city? No crowds were gathering. At length we questioned a passer by, and received for answer, "It is ringing because an Apprentice is out of his time." "Out of his time!" We knew nothing of the boy, neither his name or home, but the waves of air told us something concerning him. We knew he had overcome difficulties, often had he been disheartened and dismayed, often had he heard the mocking laugh or coarse jest of his companions, at his imperfect workmanship, often heard the angry words over goods or tools spoiled through his ignorance or carelessness. He had risen on dark mornings when his neighbors, lads his own age, were snugly sleeping; he had toiled on glorious summer days when his indolent companions were resting under green trees, or plunging into the cool waters; he had done the rough work because he was "the boy." Yes, but there is another side to the picture. With courage renewed, with eyes and fingers becoming more and more accustomed to the handicrafts of his trade, every month has found him progressing, till to-night, as the still ringing bell tells us, he has overcome. His companions gather around him with boisterous mirth, and the "older hands" feel a certain pride in him, as wringing his hand they know he ranks among themselves, the means of an honest living at his disposal, one of God's great army of working men. A few hours passed and another bell resounded upon our ears. We listened, for that bell had a sad and solemn sound. Ah, another "Apprentice was out of his time." We knew something of how he had fought, not with rough iron, but with "the waves of this troublesome world." We knew how in every day life he strove to do his duty to his Lord and Master. Dismayed, how often? Discouraged, how frequently bearing the taunt, the sneer? But he too had overcome. His companions gather around him, but all mirth is hushed, tears fill their eyes, and choking words are whispered as they file round the casket, and look upon the calm dead face, that no more on earth will meet them with its wonted smile, and the pale hands that have done all their rough earthwork. His welcome we did not hear. Ah, it is well that the sound of harps and the silvery peals from the chiming bells of the city of God reach us not, or perchance we should "stand all the day idle." For are we not all entered Apprentices in this strange world of ours? Are we not all "serving our time?" How are we learning our trades? Are we likely to prove "workmen that need not be ashamed," or are we through fear or negligence hiding in the earth our Lord's money? Our indentures bear the blood-red seals of Calvary, our Covenant is "ordered in all things and sure." The time of our serving here is unknown to us, of the hour of our release knoweth no man. There have been some who "being made perfect in a short time, fullfilled for a long time." We have a long line of witnesses gone on before, but all drawing their life and courage from that Wonderful Man, the Redeemer of the world, the Carpenter of Galilee. He whose mysterious indentures were cancelled in the noon-day of His life. He who could stand among His sorrowing companions and say, "Father, I have finished the work which Thou gavest me to do." Oh, my fellow apprentices, how often are we tempted to leave *our* work unfinished. Do we not thus sometimes think, "I can never learn my trade for heaven here." We see one wasting his Master's goods, we see the tables of the money-changers in the temple of God, we hear our fellows arraigning the Master before their petty tribunals, we grow faint and weary, we have foes within and without. Doubt says, "The Master is feasting royally and forgets his poor apprentices." Courage, courage, my brothers, we are treading the path the saints have trod. This is but a state of preparation. We know not what work for the King we may have to do by-and-by; over how many cities of whose locality we at present know nothing. He may give us authority to which of the countless worlds in our Father's universe we may be sent on the King's message of love, to what spirits in prison we, in our spiritual life, may go to preach of mercy. If here permitted to be the servants of Christ, and through His merits attaining to that better country, may we not reasonably infer that we shall aid Him more and more, till the mediatorial work is ended. Let these thoughts encourage us amidst the cold and heat, the scorn and shame. Let us see to it that we *do* work the works of our Master. Let us often turn our eyes to those two grand rules of our workshop, "Do unto others as ye would they should do unto you," our golden rule framed in the royal crimson of the King's authority; and that other silver lettered motto, framed in the clear, true blue of heaven, "Pure religion and undefiled before God and the Father, is to visit the widow and fatherless in their affliction, and to keep himself unspotted from the world." Let us imitate that brother workman of whom Whittier says:

> "He gave up his life to others,
>   Himself to his brothers lending;
> He saw the Lord in His suffering brothers,
>   And not in the clouds descending."

Soon, soon we shall be out of our time; but here the figure ends. The earthly apprentice, freed from his articles of apprenticeship, may serve any master, the heavenly apprentice asks but *one*. Oh, Jesus, Master, Thou Saviour of our race, have mercy upon us, grant us so to serve Thee in time, that our earthly labours ended, we may hear Thee say, "Well done good and faithful servant," while the pure and beautiful angels shall rehearse to each other, "Rejoice, another apprentice is out of his time."

Two Altars.

"And Cain talked with Abel, his brother."

The sun was rising on earth, sin-tainted, yet beautiful,
Delicate gold-colored cloudlets in all their primeval beauty,
Ushered the bright orb of day to his task well appointed,
Like a bevy of beautifal girls in the court of their monarch,
Or a regiment of soldiers all bright in new rose-colored armour.
Two altars arose between earth and the cloud-speckled firmament;
Cain walked in a stern and defiant advance to his altar,
A recklessness flashed from his eyes, and passions unconquered,
As he scornfully looked on the kneeling, worshipping Abel,
Ay scornfully thus he addressed his young innocent brother:

"Look at my sacrifice, Abel, these glistening dew-colored roses,
Those delicate lillies and mosses, these graceful arbutulas;
Look at the golden brown tints of these fruits in their lusciousness; '
Look at the bright varied hues of these green leaves, closely encircling
These rich scarlet blossoms, like yonder clouds, glorious and wonderful;
Nothing on earth or in heaven could make fairer oblation.
Abel, what have you carved on your altar, in that wild devotion
By which you in vain seek to soften the anger of heaven?
A circle, to show that your God is all near, is filling
The seen and unseen with His incomprehensible presence.

Well, so let it be, then; I'll not contradict the illusion.
One thing appears certain, that we have offended our Maker,
Who visits unjustly on us the mistakes of our parents,
As if we ever reached out our hands for fruit once forbidden.
Shall we never be free from the thorns and the thistles upspringing?
Why do you still try to follow the steps and voice of your Maker?
And why still persist in slaying the white lambs of your meadows?
Take of my beautiful flowers and despise all blood shedding."

"My brother," spoke Abel, "I love the dear innocent flowers,
Are they not all, nearly all that is left us of Eden's fair glory,
All but the singing of birds, the winds and the waters, wild music,
All but the whispers of love and blessings of heart-broken parents;
But you heard, my brother, as well as myself the commandment,
Not to offer to heaven what *we* choose, but what God declareth
Will shadow our Faith and sweet Hope in the promised atonement;
And that terrible sin, those spots in our souls, my dear brother,
Can never be cleansed by the lives of the beautiful flowers,
Only by His, shadowed forth in the death of an innocent victim."

Then angrily answered Cain back to his young brother's pleading,
"Abel, I have no patience with such mock humiliations,
I have no need of a Saviour, I have no need of blood-shedding
To wash out the stain of my own or my father's transgression.
I for myself can make perfect and full restitution;
Look at the smoke of your altar curling upward so clearly,
Making white cloudlets on high in the blue of the firmament,
While mine sweeps the ground that is cursed like the trail of the serpent:
Why comes down the Maker of this blighted universe, asking
Why art thou wroth, and why is thy countenance fallen?"

Stand I not here in the image of God, who created us?
Have I not courage, and freedom, and strength above my inferiors?
Did not our father give name to beast, bird, insect and reptile?
Shall his children crouch down and kneel like the creature that crawleth?
I will not obey this commandment, but I'll wreath up my altar
With offerings of earth, with gold of the orange, and red of the roses,
I'll not stain my hands with the blood of an innocent creature."
So Cain turned away from his wondering brother; perhaps then little dreaming
That on the next morrow he would become earth's first murderer;
And, scorning the death of a lamb, take the life of a brother.

The Doom of Cain.

The Lord Said, "What hast thou done?"

  Oh, erring Cain,
What hast thou done? Upon the blighted earth
I hear a melancholy wail resounding;
Among the blades of grass where flowers have birth
I hear a new-born tone mournfully sounding.
  It is thy brother's blood
   Crying aloud to God
    In helpless pain.

  Unhappy Cain!
Thou hast so loved to wreathe the clinging vine,
And welcomed with pure joy the delicate fruit,
Till thou hast felt a kindred feeling twine
Around thy heart, grown with each fibrous root
  Of tree, or moss, or flower,
   Growing in field or bower,
    Or ripening grain.

  But henceforth, Cain,
When the bright gleaming of the rosy morn
Proclaims another glorious summer day,
Thou may'st walk forth to greet the earth newborn,
And pluck the blushing roses on thy way;
  They at thy touch shall blight,
   Stricken with some strange might,
    Some dire pain.

  In time to come,
When thy fair child (for thou shalt have a son)
Shall lay his little, soft, warm hands in thine,
And say, "My father, growing neath the sun
Are lovely flowers, trees and moss and vine;
  Here is rich soil and room
   For me; make bowers bloom
    Around our home."

  Thy heart will shrink,
And thou wilt hear the voice the Lord has heard,
The voice of brother's blood speaking from earth,
And each pulse of thy sad soul will be stirred,
As he to whom the girl thou love'st gave birth

   Brings back with fearful truth
   The playmate of thy youth
     From the grave's brink.

     For on no shore
Shall fair earth yield unto thy stalwart arms;
No, thou may'st dig, and prune, and plant in vain,
And noxious worms and things of poisonous harms
Shall not be banished at the will of Cane;
   Thou'lt set seed-bearing root,
   Thou'lt plant life-giving fruit
     No more, no more.

     Depart! Depart!
Ah no, not greater than the soul can bear,
Did'st thou not always find whatever grain
Thou cast, the same grew upward full and fair,
Thou *would'st not* look upon the pure lamb slain,
   To faith true sacrifice
   Thou would'st not turn thine eyes;
     Go, till thine heart.

Our Poor Brethren.

> "Our poor and penniless brethren, dispersed over land and sea."--Masonic Sentiment

They met in the festive hall,
  Lamps in their brightness shone,
And merry music and mirth,
  Aided the feast of St. John.
Men pledged the health of their Queen
  And of all the Royal band,
The flags of a thousand years,
  The swords of their motherland.

Then mid the revelry came
  The sound of a mournful strain,
Like a minor chord in music,
  A sweet but sad refrain;
It rose on the heated air,
  Like a mourner's earnest plea,
"Our poor and penniless brethren
  Dispersed over land and sea."

Poor and penniless brethren
  Scattered over the world,
Want and misfortune and woe
  Round them fierce darts have hurled;
Wandering alone upon mountains,
  Sick and fainting and cold,
Lying heart-broken in prisons,
  Chained in an enemy's hold.

Dying in fields of combat,
  With none to answer back
The masonic sign of distress,
  Left on the battle's track
Shipwrecked in foaming waters,
  Clinging to broken spars,
Dying, this night of St. John,
  Mid the ocean and the stars.

Others with hunger faint--we
  Taste these rich and varied meats--
Oppression gives them no home
  But dark and desolate streets.

Oh, God of mercy, hear us,
  As we ask a boon for Thee,
For poor and penniless brethren
  Dispersed over land and sea.

Poor and penniless brethren,
  Ah, in the Master's sight,
We all lay claim to the title
  On this, our festival night.
Lone pilgrims journeying on
  Towards light that points above,
Treading the chequered earthworks
  Till we reach the land of love.

Work up to the landmark, brothers,
  We shall not always stay,
The falling shadows warn us
  To work in the light of day.
How often our footsteps turn
  Where a brother's form is hid,
Oft we cast evergreen sprigs
  On a brother's coffin lid.

Thou, who dost give to each
  Some appointed post to hold,
Teach us to cherish the weak,
  To give Thy silver and gold;
To guard as a soldier guards
  Honor and Love's pure shrine,
To give our lives for others,
  As Thou did'st for us give Thine.

To Masons all over the world
  Give wisdom to work aright,
That they may gather in peace
  Their working tools at night.
May love's star glitter o'er each,
  Amid darkness, storm or mist,
As on this night of St. John,
  Our Blest Evangelist.

Vain Dreams.

>--"Throughout the day, I walk,
>My path o'ershadowed by vain dreams of him."
>--Italian Girl's Hymn to the Virgin.

Mother, gazing on thy son,
He, thy precious only one,
Look into his azure eyes,
Clearer than the summer skies.
Mark his course; on scrolls of fame
Read his proud ancestral name;
Pause! a cloud that path will dim,
Thou hast dreamt vain dreams of him.

Young bride, for the altar crowned,
Now thy lot with one is bound,
Will *he* keep each solemn vow?
Will *he* ever love as now?
Ah! a dreamy shadow lies
In the depths of those bright eyes;
Time will this day's glory dim,
Thou hast dreamt vain dreams of him.

Sister, has thy brother gone,
To the fields where fights are won;
Oh! it was an hour of pride
When he was last by thy side;
Thou dost see him coming back
In the conqueror's proud track;
Hush! the bayonets earthward turn,
Dream vain dreams, he'll not return.

Woman, on the cottage green,
Gazing at the sunset scene,
Now the vintage toil is o'er,
But the gleaner comes no more
Through the fields of burnished corn;
Lo! a peasant's bier is borne
By the sparkling river's brim,
Thou hast dreamt vain dreams of him.

Maiden, who in every prayer
Breath'st a name thou dost not bear,
Sing again thy lover's song;

Yes, he will be back ere long,
Back in all his manhood's pride,
Back, but with another bride;
Cease those bridal robes to trim,
Thou hast dreamt vain dreams of him.

Earthly idols! how we mould
Sand with fruit and clay with gold!
How we cherish crumbling dust,
Then lament our futile trust!
Saviour, who on earth didst prove
All the agony of love,
Fit us for that brighter shore,
Where they dream vain dreams no more.

The Forest River.

Amid the forest verdant shade,
    A peaceful river flowed:
Wild flowers their home on its banks had made,
The sunbeam's rays on its breast were laid,
    When the light of morning glowed.

By its marge the wolf had found a lair,
    He roamed through each lonely spot;
That deep designer, the beaver, there
Built his palace; the shaggy bear
    In the tall tree had his cot.

And voices sweet were heard on the bank
    Of the river's gentle flow;
The whip-poor-will sang when the sun had sank,
And the hum-drum bee to his home had shrank,
    When the wind of eve did blow.

The tree-frog joined with his sonorous call,
    The grasshopper chirped along,
The dormice came out of their underground hole,
The squirrels peeped over their pine-tree wall,
    To list to the revel song.

Nothing disturbed the murmur deep
    Of the river broad and fair;
No one awoke it from peaceful sleep,
Save when floating mice o'er its breast would creep,
    Or the rusty-coated bear.

One morn the sound of an axe was heard
    In the forest, dark and lone;
Then started with fear the beasts disturbed,
Their reign was broke at the woodman's word,
    And they scowled with anger on.

On the river's brink the emigrant's child
    Passed all his lonely hours,
He laughed when he ruffled the bosom mild
Of the flowing streamlet so bright and wild,
    As it bore his boon of flowers.

Soon the throng of the forest heard the horn
    Of the boat, the commerce boat;
Then they started up from the brake and thorn,

And hastening away by the light of the morn,
   They fled from cavern and moat.

And the bird peeped out of a pine tree tower,
   And shrank away at the sight,
The humming-bird fled to his rose-hung bower,
The bright bee curled himself snug in a flower,
   O'ertaken by fear and fright.

And the river which rolled for ages, still
   In a gentle flow unriven,
Now bears on its bosom by man's proud will,
By the arts of industry and skill,
   The blessings to mortals given.

Over its billows the steamboats tread,
   With their waters rushing high,
Or the snowy sail to the wind is spread,
As the noble bark on her way is sped
   To the crowded city nigh.

Oh river bright, we sail over thy breast,
   Once bearing wood runners wild;
But the birds who built on the bank their nest,
Have fled long ago to the boundless west,
   From thee and from man exiled.

Last Words of Sir Henry Lawrence.

"Let there be no fuss about me, bury me with my men."

The shades of death were gathering thick around a soldier's head,
A war stained, dust strewn band of men gathered around his bed.
"Comrade, good-bye; thank God your voice may cheer the dauntless brave
When I, your friend and countryman, am resting in the grave.
Hush, soldiers, hush, no word of thanks, it is little I have done
For the glory of the land we love, toward the setting sun.
I have but one request to make: When all is over, then
Let there be no fuss about me, bury me with my men.

Heap up no splendid monument in memory of my clay,
No tributary words to tell of one who's far away;
It matters not to passers by where lies my crumbling dust,
The cherubim and seraphim may have it in their trust;
And bones of better men than I have bleached all cold and white
Where scorching sunbeam goes by day and the prowling beast by night.
Give me a few spare feet of earth away down in the glen,
Breathing the words of faith and hope, bury me with the men.

Bury me with the men; when the fearful seige was gained,
With British blood and British dead the Indian soil was stained.
Poor Dugald lay that fearful night and never asked for aid,
And Fraser, wounded, cheered us on, and Allan, dying, prayed,
And brave Macdonald cheered the flag with his expiring breath.
These are the men who jeopardised their lives unto the death,
They drove the murderous Sepoys back, the wild wolf to his den;
All honor to their noble hearts; bury me with my men.

Is it death that's coming nearer? how clammy grows my brow;
Yes, I'm going home for promotion, the battle's over now.
Comrades, I often fancy, how upon yon blessed shore,
In that land of recognition, we may yet all meet once more.
Colonel, we'll gather round you then, as in the days of old;
Why do whisper, comrades, are my fingers growing cold?
Oh, tell my brother-officers that I thought about them when
I was going across the river; bury me with my men.

How very dark it's growing, I suppose it's nearly night;
Well, I think we shall see England in the morning's ruddy light.
And my mother and my sister surely I see them stand
Upon the beach, and summer flowers waving in each hand;
And sounds of joy and victory comes on the evening air.

Colonel, if I go down home first, you'll come and see us there?
Do I hear my comrades sighing? Where am I? ah, amen.
Let there be no fuss about me, bury me with my men.

To the Birds.

Onward, sail on in your boundless flight,
Neath shadowing skies and moonbeams bright,
Kissing the clouds as it drops the rain,
Touching the wall of the rainbow's fane;
With your wings unfurled, your lyres strung,
You sail where stars in their orbs are hung,
Or for stranger lands where bright flow'rs spring,
Ye have plumed the down and spread the wing.

We lay the strength of the forest down,
We wear the robe and the shining crown,
We tread down kings in our battle path,
And voices fail at our gathered wrath;
We touch; the numbers forget to pour,
From the serpent's hiss to the lion's roar;
But we may not tread the paths ye've trod,
Though children of men and sons of God.

Ye haste, ye haste, but ye bring not back
To waiting spirits the news we lack,
Ye do not tell what it is to see
The snow capped home of the thunder free,
Ye do not speak of the worlds above,
Ye tell no tales of the things we love,
No height or breadth of the sunbeam's roof,
You touch in your travels--terror proof.

You're strange in bright radience, wonderful;
You're soft in your plumage, beautiful.
Bold to bask in the clouds of even,
Free in your flight to floors of heaven.
Like dews that over the flowers spring,
Like billows rolled over Egypt's king,
You leave no track in the misty air,
Or records of wonders that meet you there.

Initiation Ode.

Air--Belmont.

Hark! unto thee a voice doth speak,
　A voice of heavenly breath,
And this, the solemn charge it gives,
　Be faithful unto death.

Faithful as stars in heaven's blue skies,
　Though dark clouds roll between,
Or rocks that show their signal lights
　In tempest's wildest scene.

Faithful 'till death, which finally
　Shall close thy mortal strife,
When thy reward shall surely be
　The crown of endless life.

Installation Ode.

Blest Ruler, at whose word
The universe was stirred,
  And there was light;
Look now with gracious love
From Thy bright home above,
Direct in every move,
  Each proved, Sir Knight.

In mysteries well skilled,
Their hearts with courage filled,
  Behold they stand;
Strengthen their faith in thee,
Let hope their anchor be,
And heaven-born charity
  Mark their command.

Endure with holy light
Each suppliant, Sir Knight;
  May each one prove
Faithful in watch and word;
Strong the oppressed, to guard
And win the just reward
  Of Faith and Love.

Milton Keynes UK
Ingram Content Group UK Ltd.
UKHW030955261124
451585UK00005B/731